P9-CEN-622

TOUCH THE BRIGHTEST STAR

Christie Matheson

GREENWILLOW BOOKS

An Imprint of HarperCollinsPublishers

Touch the Brightest Star
Copyright © 2015 by Christie Matheson.
All rights reserved. Manufactured in China.
For information address HarperCollins Children's Books,
a division of HarperCollins Publishers,
195 Broadway, New York, NY 10007.
www.harpercollinschildrens.com

Collages were used to prepare the full-color art.
The text type is 30-point Stempel Schneidler.

Library of Congress Cataloging-in-Publication Data

Matheson, Christie, author, illustrator.
Touch the brightest star / Christie Matheson.
pages cm
"Greenwillow Books."
Summary: An interactive picture book showcasing the beauty of nighttime.
ISBN 978-0-06-227447-2 (trade ed.)
[1. Bedtime—Fiction. 2. Night—Fiction.] I. Title.
PZ8.3.M4227 To 2015 [E]—dc23 2014030491

First Edition
15 16 17 18 19 SCP 10 9 8 7 6 5 4 3 2 1

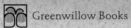 Greenwillow Books

For Will

Magic happens every night.
First wave good-bye to the sun's bright light.

Gently press the firefly.

Oh!

Press again to light up the sky.

Now let's blow a quiet breeze.

Pat the deer

and say good night, please.

Tap the sky beside the tree.

Make a wish and count to three.

Swipe the sky

from left to right.

Wow!

Now blink your eyes. . . .

What a starry night!

Touch the brightest star you see.
Psst.
It's right there, near the tree.

Trace the picture of the dipper.
(That's a kind of spoon.)

Look! A little one!

Time to whisper,
"Come out, moon!"

Watch the sky and call,
"Whoo! Whoo!"

Then turn the page to see who's new.

Rub the owls on their heads.

It's their turn to fly to bed.

Close your eyes and breathe in deeply.

Nod your head if you feel sleepy.

Shhhhh.

When you open your eyes again . . .

the magic of the day begins.

HOW THE MAGIC HAPPENS

What we see at night looks magical,
but there's a reason for everything.

FIREFLIES have special light-making organs in their bodies. They flash their lights to attract friends.

WHITE-TAILED DEER often eat at dusk, when there is still some light in the sky. They like to eat plants, including the leaves of birch trees.

STARS are huge balls of hot plasma. Most are very, very far away from Earth and look like tiny spots of light in the night sky.

A **METEOR** is often called a "shooting star." But it is actually the streak of light from a small space rock that's burning up as it travels through the Earth's layers of air.

The **BIG DIPPER** and **LITTLE DIPPER** are patterns of stars. The Big Dipper is shaped like a ladle, or large spoon, and the Little Dipper is shaped like a smaller ladle.

OWLS are nocturnal birds. That means they are active at night. An owl's call is known as a **hoot**, and it often sounds like this: "Whoo!"

The **MOON** travels around the Earth. It glows because the sun is shining on it. Sometimes the sun only shines on part of the moon, so it might look like a crescent in the sky. And sometimes the sun shines on the whole face of the moon. That's when it looks like a circle and is called a full moon.

MORNING GLORIES and **POPPIES** are flowers that close at night and open in the morning.